To Lexus

FROM
GREAT GRANDPA +
GRANDAA KOMMER

To Lexus

FROM

ANGELINA KATRINA

Bugs In My Backyard

In the beautiful city of Bluffton, South Carolina, there lived a very kind little girl named Angelina Katrina. She loved bugs and butterflies. She would spend many hours looking at them. This is Angelina Katrina's story about the bugs in her backyard.

D W PUBLISHING
Dan Waltz
www.dwpublishing.com
(810) 695-8985
U.S.A.

Printed in Hong Kong

ISBN: 0-9741774-4-X

Kathleen Loper
Author
Loper Tales
2391 Beech Drive
Kawkawlin, MI 48631
www.lopertales.com
(989) 671-8211

Dan Waltz
Artist/Illustrator
D.W. Publishing
226 Mcfarland Street
Grand Blanc, MI 48439
www.DanWaltz.com
(810) 695-8985

One sunny day while Angelina Katrina
was playing in her backyard, she saw a fuzzy
wuzzy bumblebee on the petal of a flower.
Angelina Katrina smiled and said,
"Good morning Mr. Bee." And he replied:

"My color is black and yellow
I'm a happy sort of fellow.
I pollinate the flowers
And I buzz around for hours.
I am Buzz the Bumblebee."

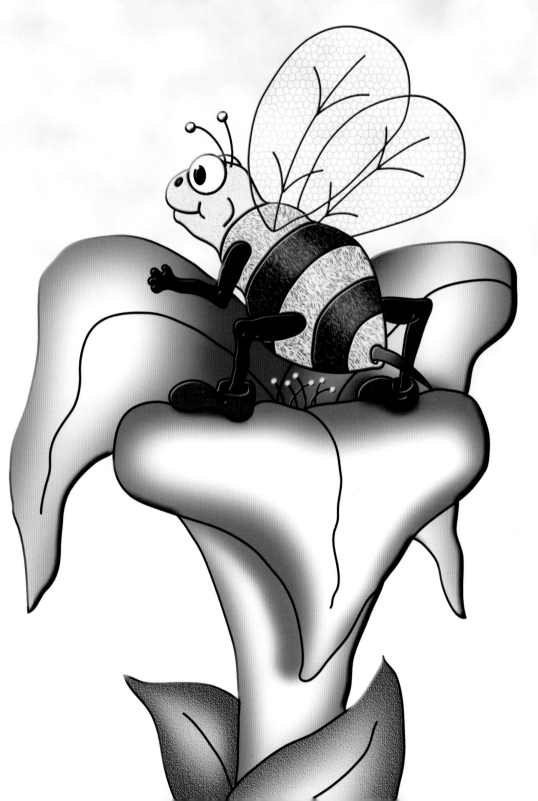

Angelina Katrina then
found a wiggly worm
crawling on top of the ground.
She picked him up
and he said to her:

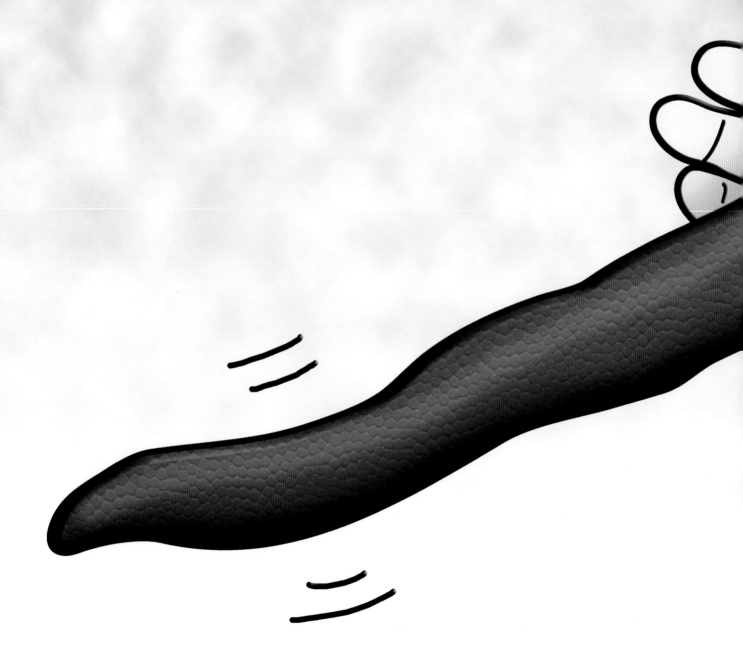

"I like to squirm and wiggle
I make little kids giggle.
I live beneath the ground
But I never make a sound
I am Earl the Earthworm."

Later on that day, Angelina Katrina
saw a tiny snail slowly moving on the ground.
When Angelina Katrina took a closer look,
she heard him say:

"I move about very slow
But I get where I want to go.
I like to play in the sun
But I still get my work done
I am Shane the Snail."

Angelina Katrina was playing in her backyard
when she saw a little bug asleep on a plant.
As she softly touched it, the little bug said:

"I like to rest during the day
While all of the other bugs play.
I'm so colorful and bright
My body glows at night.
I'm Leela the Lightning Bug."

Angelina Katrina
was walking in her backyard
when she saw a black ant
carrying a big piece of bread.
The black ant told her:

"You'll never hear an ant
ever say the words, I can't.
I work very hard all day
I spend little time to play.
I am Annie the Ant."

While Angelina Katrina was playing
in her backyard, she saw
something crawling.
As she reached out
and touched it she
heard it say:

"I am very fuzzy and long
And I cannot sing a song.
I grow into a butterfly
And I fly up to the sky.
I am Casey the Caterpillar."

Angelina Katrina was out in
her backyard when a black and red bug
lit upon her arm and said:

"They call me the lady bug
My shell fits me very snug.
I am red with some black spots
And they look like polka dots.
I am Lisa the Ladybug."

Angelina Katrina was swinging
in her backyard when a bug
flew upon her hand and said:

"I like to flutter all about
I have a very long snout.
My colors are oh so bright
Don't worry for I do not bite.
I am Daisy the Dragonfly."

Angelina Katrina was sitting out in her backyard that evening when she heard something chirp and say:

"Listen to me chirp and sing
With the flutter of my wings.
I make a loud and funny noise
Just to amuse the girls and boys.
I am Chad the Cricket."

Angelina Katrina was so excited and happy about meeting the many bug friends in her back yard.

She wanted to share her new bug friends with her people friends, so Angelina Katrina had a party and invited some of her friends. They played bug games and people games and everybody had so much fun.

Bugs In My Backyard

"My color is black and yellow
I'm a happy sort of fellow.
I pollinate the flowers
And I buzz around for hours.
I am Buzz the Bumblebee."

"I like to squirm and wiggle
I make little kids giggle.
I live beneath the ground
But I never make a sound
I am Earl the Earthworm."

"I move about very slow
But I get where I want to go.
I like to play in the sun
But I still get my work done
I am Shane the Snail."

"I like to rest during the day
While all of the other bugs play.
I'm so colorful and bright
My body glows at night.
I'm Leela the Lightning Bug."

"You'll never hear an ant
ever say the words, I can't.
I work very hard all day
I spend little time to play.
I am Annie the Ant."

"I am very fuzzy and long
And I cannot sing a song.
I grow into a butterfly
And I fly up to the sky.
I am Casey the Caterpillar."

"They call me the lady bug
My shell fits me very snug.
I am red with some black spots
And they look like polka dots.
I am Lisa the Ladybug."

"I like to flutter all about
I have a very long snout.
My colors are oh so bright
Don't worry for I do not bite.
I am Daisy the Dragonfly."

"Listen to me chirp and sing
With the flutter of my wings.
I make a loud and funny noise
Just to amuse the girls and boys.
I am Chad the Cricket."

-Kathleen Loper-

Kathleen Loper, Author

Born in Bay City, Michigan in 1940 and resided there most of her life. She loves American and English Literature and began writing poetry when she was a teenager. She developed a habit of writing short stories during her travels to Singapore - Paris, France - Zurich, Switzerland - Istanbul, Turkey and Bombay, India.

She was blessed with three wonderful children: Robert, Vicki and Randy, five marvelous grandchildren and a precious great-granddaughter named Angelina, who was and still continues to be the inspiration for Kathleen's stories.

Kathleen is presently working on her next story, about Angelina Katrina building a snowman she calls Troy.

For more information visit her online...www.lopertales.com
Loper Tales • 2391 Beech Drive • Kawkawlin • MI • 48631 • (989) 671-8211

Dan Waltz, Illustrator

Award winning Michigan Wildlife Artist does many shows through out the year, selling his original life-like watercolor/acrylic paintings and prints. His work has been featured in or on covers of many publications, including "Michigan-Out-of-Doors" magazine and several Michigan area phone books. He has raised thousands of dollars with his work for non-profit organizations such as..."Ducks Unlimited", "The Bass Research Foundation", "The Humane Society" and "Tenth Life" just to name a few. He is also the illustrator for several children's books.

Dan's love for the out-doors is truly reflected in the paintings he paints. Dan is also a graphic designer and has been since 1980. He produces 4 color catalogs, advertisements, brochures, digital photo-retouching/restoration, web design and illustration. All of which has lead him to open his own business, D. W. Publishing (www.dwpublishing.com) where he illustrates and publishes books and art prints.

For more information visit his website at...www.DanWaltz.com
D.W. Publishing • 226 McFarland Street • Grand Blanc • MI • 48439 • (810) 695-8985 • Email: Dan@dwpublishing.com